Hissss!

Mick Inkpen

Hodder
Children's
Books

A division of Hodder Headline Limited

The sun was making
a shadow of Kipper
on the wall.
It was a hot day.
A very hot day.

Kipper lay on his blanket, and sucked his drink through a curly-wurly straw.

'Today is a paddling pool kind of day,' he said.

The paddling pool
was on the top shelf
of the toy cupboard.

Kipper grabbed it and
pulled enthusiastically.

The toys in the cupboard
fell on Kipper's head.

Ouch!

I t was hard work
blowing up the
paddling pool.
　So when Kipper was
finished, he turned on
the hose and went to
buy an ice cream.

On the way back
the ice cream
melted down Kipper's
paw, and plopped into
a puddle.

'That's odd,' said
Kipper. 'It wasn't
raining when I left.'

The puddle was as big as a pond. In the middle was Kipper's paddling pool looking very saggy.

'I know what has happened,' said Kipper.

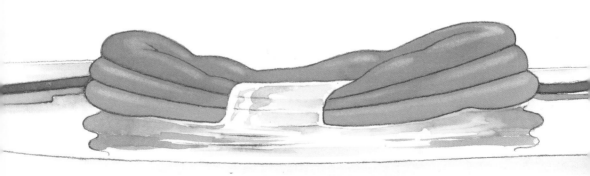

K ipper knelt down
and listened very
carefully to the
paddling pool.

   With his big ears he
could just hear a
tiny,

   tiny

      hissss
            s s s s s s
                  s s s s s s s
                      s s s s s s s s
                          s s s s s s s s s s s

ssssss!

K ipper took the sticking plaster from his head.

Ouch!

And he mended the paddling pool . . .

. . .which was clever,
wasn't it?

First published 1999
by Hodder Children's Books,
a division of Hodder Headline Limited
338 Euston Road, London NW1 3BH

Copyright © Mick Inkpen 1999

10   9

ISBN 0 340 736917

Printed in Hong Kong